For Gemk,

Whose endless supply of ideas and honest critique made this possible.

感謝 Gemk

源源不絕的靈感及誠懇的建議讓這一切成真。

The Zombies Go To the Zoo

小殭屍逛動物園

Coleen Reddy 著

李超美 繪

薛慧儀 譯

三民書局

Zack was a zombie.

He was not a zealous zombie because he did not enjoy scaring people.

A good zombie was a zombie that could scare people.

柴克是一個殭屍。

但他不是一個愛嚇人的殭屍，他對「嚇人」這事兒興趣缺缺。

可是，只有會嚇人的殭屍，才是好的殭屍。

At zombie school the zombies learned how to scare people.

小殭屍們在殭屍學校裡學習如何去嚇人。

First, they learned how to make strange noises and laugh in an evil way.
When people laughed it's: "HA HA HA!"
When zombies laughed it's: "HEE HEE HEE!"

首先，他們要學會發出怪異的聲音和邪惡的笑聲。
人的笑聲是「哈哈哈！」，但殭屍笑起來卻是「嘻嘻嘻！」

7

Then zombies learned a very important lesson.
They learned how to say: "BOO!"
Zack knew how to do the zombie laugh and how to say: "BOO!"

接著，小殭屍們要上一門很重要的課。
那就是如何發出「怖」的嚇人聲音。
柴克已經學會了如何發出殭屍的笑聲和「怖」的聲音。

9

But that wasn't all.

Zombies had to learn how to make their eyes pop out of their heads.

The really good zombies could make their brains pop out of their heads.

They did this to scare people. If you couldn't do this,

then you couldn't really scare people.

但這還不是全部喔！
小殭屍們還必須學會如何把眼球瞪出眼眶來。
真正厲害的殭屍，還可以把腦子從頭裡面給蹦出來呢！
他們就是靠這些伎倆來嚇人，如果不會這些的話，就嚇不倒人囉！

But no matter how hard he tried,
Zack could not make his eyes or brains pop out.
His teacher gave him big, fat zeroes
and Zack had to spend another year in the third grade.

但柴克不管怎麼努力，就是沒有辦法把眼睛或是腦子給蹦出來。
老師給了他圓圓胖胖的大鴨蛋，柴克只得再讀一次三年級。

One night, the teacher took the students to the zoo.
Zombies did everything at night, so they went to the zoo at night.
The students went every year.

有天晚上，老師帶學生們到動物園去。
殭屍不管做什麼事都在晚上，所以他們也在晚上去動物園。
殭屍學校的學生每年都會去一趟動物園。

They would run around scaring the animals in their cages. They had to practice scaring animals before they could scare people.

他們到處跑來跑去，去嚇那些被關在籠子裡的動物。
他們在可以嚇人之前必須先練習嚇動物。

17

The students were standing outside the zebra cage
and pulling faces at the zebras.
They made their scary noises and did their evil zombie laugh.

他們站在斑馬籠子前，
對斑馬做鬼臉，
並且發出可怕的聲音和邪惡的殭屍笑聲。

One zebra got so scared that it ran into the shadows
and hid from the zombies.
Next, the zombies went to scare the lions.
Zack just walked off by himself.

有一隻斑馬因為太害怕，跑到暗處躲了起來。
接著殭屍們又跑去嚇獅子，但柴克卻獨自走開了。

21

He walked for a few minutes before he heard something running towards him. He saw all the students screaming and running in a zigzag.
"What is it?" he asked them.
"Run! Save yourself. It's a vicious lion on the loose!" yelled the students.

他走了幾分鐘後，聽見有東西正向他跑過來。

他看見所有的同學都在尖叫，而且像無頭蒼蠅一樣四處逃竄。

「怎麼啦？」他問他們。

「快跑呀！不然你就死定了！有一隻兇猛的獅子跑出籠子了！」同學們喊著。

In a minute the students had all run away
and Zack was still standing there.
He was about to turn and run when he saw something.
It was not a vicious lion, but a little lion cub.
It wasn't roaring, but crying.

所有的學生一下子都跑光了，只剩下柴克還站在那裡。

他正想轉身逃跑時，看見了一個東西。

那不是什麼兇猛的獅子，只是隻小獅子嘛！

而且牠不是在怒吼，而是在大哭呢！

"Please help me, I can't find my family. I'm lost," said the lion cub.
"I asked your friends for help but when they saw me, they ran away.
Help me find my parents. They'll be so happy to see me.
They'll do anything for you."
"Anything?" asked Zack, with a naughty look on his face.
"Can your parents pretend to be scared?"

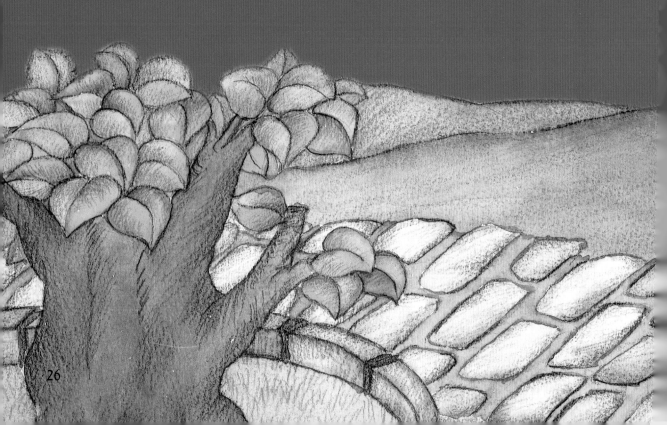

「請你幫幫我，我找不到我的家人！我迷路了！」小獅子說。
「我想請你的朋友幫忙，可是他們一看見我就全跑光了。
請幫我找到爸爸媽媽好不好？他們看到我一定會很高興的，
然後就會答應為你做任何事情。」
「任何事情嗎？」柴克問，露出頑皮的表情。
「那，你的爸爸媽媽可不可以假裝被嚇倒呀？」

The students were waiting for Zack when he ran back to them.
"Are you okay?" they asked. "Did the terrible lion bite you?"
"Bite me? Are you kidding? Lions are afraid of me!" said Zack.

柴克跑回來的時候，所有的同學都在等他。
他們問：「你沒事吧？那隻可怕的獅子有沒有咬你啊？」
柴克說：「咬我？開玩笑！獅子怕死我了呢！」

"What did you say? Lions are afraid of you? You can't even make your eyes pop out of your head," said the students.
"I don't have to do anything. All I have to do is look at them and they go bananas," said Zack. "You can come and take a look if you want."

「你說什麼？獅子怕你？你連把眼睛蹦出來都不會呢！」其他同學說。

「我什麼都不用做，只要看著牠們，牠們就嚇壞了。」柴克說。

「不然，你們可以過來看看啊！」

The students all walked over to the lion cage.
Then Zack just looked at the lions and they really did get scared.

所有的學生都走到獅子籠前面。
結果柴克只抬眼看了看，獅子們就真的被嚇壞了！

They screamed and yelled and ran in circles.
They all tried to hide behind one another.
They were so good at pretending.

獅子們開始尖叫，還不斷地繞著圈圈跑。
每隻獅子都想躲在另一隻獅子的後頭。
牠們的演技可真是精彩呢！

"Wow!" said the teacher. "You're a special zombie. You have a great gift.
You can scare animals just by looking at them.
You don't have to make your eyes or brains pop out of your head."

「哇！」老師說，「你真是個特別的殭屍，你有很了不起的天分。
只要看一眼就可以把動物嚇成這樣，
甚至不用把眼睛或腦子給蹦出來呢！」

"Will you let me go to the fourth grade now?" asked Zack.
"You are so gifted, you can go to the seventh grade," said the teacher.

「那麼，老師，現在你會讓我升上四年級了嗎？」柴克問。
「你這麼有天分，可以去上七年級囉！」老師說。

39

Zack was the happiest zombie.

"What assignment do I have to do in grade seven?"
Zack asked the teacher.

"You'll find it easy with your special power.

You have to scare a hundred people in one week," said the teacher.

"Oh brother!" said Zack.

現在柴克是最快樂的殭屍了。

「七年級要做什麼樣的功課呢？」柴克問老師。

「你這麼厲害，一定會覺得這項功課很容易：
只要在一個星期內嚇倒一百個人就可以了。」老師說。

「喔！天哪！」柴克說。

尋字遊戲

小朋友，想試試自己的眼力有多行嗎？現在跟我們一起來聽 CD，按下Track3，我們會把你要找的單字通通拼出來，反覆念兩次，單字的排法可能是直的或橫的，你得在我們念完之前，把所有的單字都找出來哦！

```
W S Y V I C I O U S K L
A M I B O S M I N U T E
G S C A R Y P Z F I X O
N Z         O O S P B Z
A E         R O A R C A
U B         T G R A D E
G R         A Q M T O U
H A S S I G N M E N T S
T C U C Z K T G D
Y K P R E T E N D D
I X F E V R O L P
T P R A C T I C E
A Z O M B I E N Z J M E
```

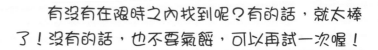

有沒有在限時之內找到呢？有的話，就太棒了！沒有的話，也不要氣餒，可以再試一次喔！

42

找到所有的單字了嗎？現在就來看看你記不記得剛剛聽過的所有單字吧！根據下面的中文意義，在圈圈內填入單字的拼法，如果拼不出來，就趕快把CD再聽一次喔！

僵屍 →〇〇〇〇〇〇

嚇人的 →〇〇〇〇〇

重要的 →〇〇〇〇〇〇〇〇〇

年級 →〇〇〇〇〇

練習 →〇〇〇〇〇〇〇〇

斑馬 →〇〇〇〇

分鐘 →〇〇〇〇〇〇

邪惡的 →〇〇〇〇〇

怒吼 →〇〇〇〇〇

淘氣的 →〇〇〇〇〇〇〇

假裝 →〇〇〇〇〇〇〇

尖叫，大叫 →〇〇〇〇〇〇

作業，功課 →〇〇〇〇〇〇〇〇

動物園 →〇〇〇

43

生字表

解答

全新創作 英文讀本
帶給你優格（yogurt）般．青春的酸甜滋味！

Teens' Chronicles

愛閱雙語叢書

青春記事簿

大維的驚奇派對／秀寶貝，說故事／杰生的大秘密
傑克的戀愛初體驗／誰是他爸爸？
叛逆大維打工記／外星老師來上課／耶！放假了！

你我身上純真的影子，
透過一篇篇幽默風趣的故事重現，
推薦你這套青春無悔的創作系列，
讓愛玫、杰生、大維、凱爾、海倫、傑克，
帶你進入他們的世界，品味另一種學習英語的全新感受。

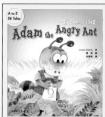

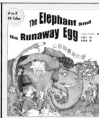

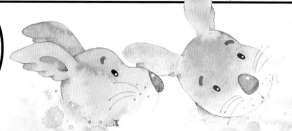

A to Z 26 Tales

二十六個妙朋友，陪你一起

愛閱雙語叢書

✿26個妙朋友系列✿

二十六個英文字母，二十六冊有趣的讀本，最適合初學英文的你！

快樂學英文！

精心錄製的雙語CD，
　　讓孩子學會正確的英文發音
用心構思的故事情節，
　　讓兒童熟悉生活中常見的單字
特別設計的親子活動，
　　讓家長和小朋友一起動動手、動動腦

中高級・中英對照
探索英文叢書

波波 唸翻天系列

你知道可愛的小兔子也會 "碎碎唸" 嗎？

波波就是這樣。

他將要告訴我們什麼有趣的故事呢？

波波的復活節／波波的西部冒險記／波波上課記／我愛你，波波
波波的下雪天／波波郊遊去／波波打球記／聖誕快樂，波波／波波的萬聖夜

共9本，每本均附CD

國家圖書館出版品預行編目資料

The Zombies Go To the Zoo：小殭屍逛動物園 /
Coleen Reddy著；李超美繪；薛慧儀譯. － －初版
一刷. － －臺北市；三民，2003
　　面；　公分 － －(愛閱雙語叢書. 二十六個妙朋
友系列) 中英對照
ISBN 957－14－3753－0　(精裝)

1.英國語言－讀本

523.38　　　　　　　　　　　　　92008791

© **The Zombies Go To the Zoo**
——小殭屍逛動物園

著作人　Coleen Reddy
繪　圖　李超美
譯　者　薛慧儀
發行人　劉振強
著作財
產權人　三民書局股份有限公司
　　　　臺北市復興北路386號
發行所　三民書局股份有限公司
　　　　地址／臺北市復興北路386號
　　　　電話／(02)25006600
　　　　郵撥／0009998－5
印刷所　三民書局股份有限公司
門市部　復北店／臺北市復興北路386號
　　　　重南店／臺北市重慶南路一段61號
初版一刷　2003年7月
編　號　S 85659－1
定　價　新臺幣壹佰捌拾元整
行政院新聞局登記證局版臺業字第○二○○號

ISBN　957－14－3753－0　　(精裝)